MORE

5-Minute
BUNNY
TALES
· for ·
Bedtime

Illustrated by Peter Stevenson

Stories by Geoffrey Cowan, Julie Good, Sue Hook,
Gabby Pritchard, Sally Sheringham, Jenny Vaughan
and Tim L West

Derrydale Books
New York · Avenel, New Jersey

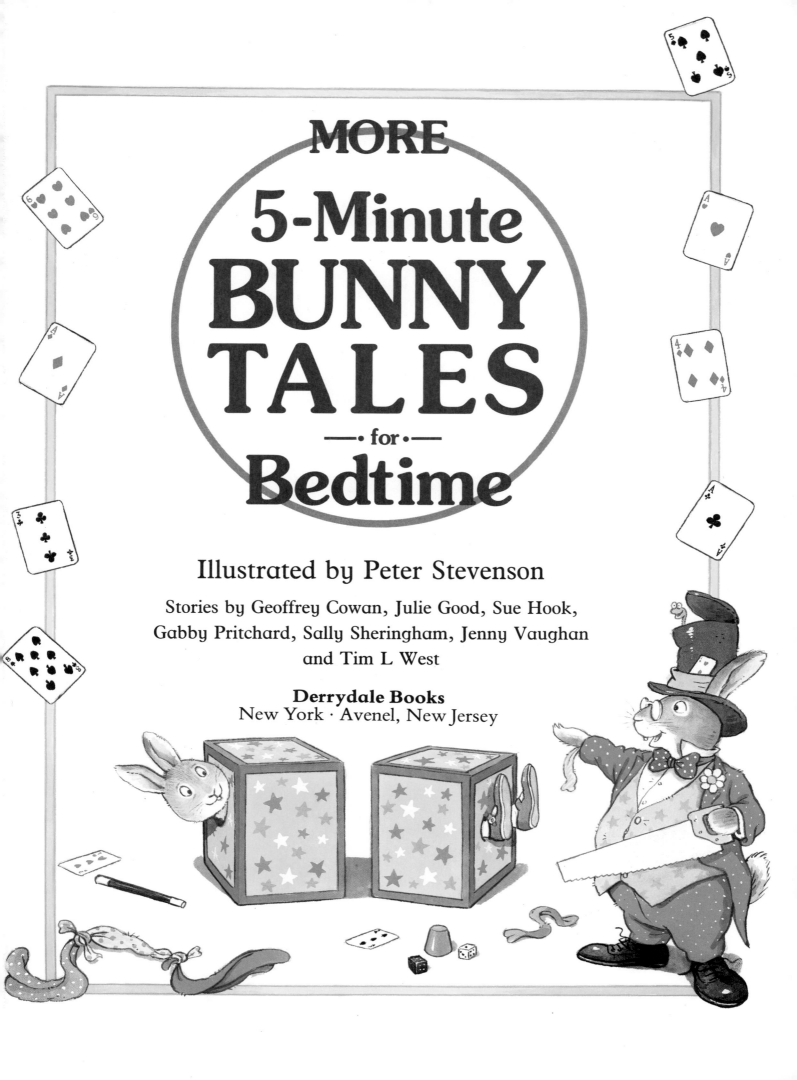

Editor: Julie Good
Production: Linda Spillane

Illustrated by Peter Stevenson

Stories by Geoffrey Cowan, Julie Good, Sue Hook, Gabby Pritchard,
Sally Sheringham, Jenny Vaughan and Tim L. West

This 1993 edition published by Derrydale Books, distributed by Outlet
Book Company, Inc., a Random House Company,
40 Engelhard Avenue, Avenel, New Jersey 07001

Random House
New York · Toronto · London · Sydney · Auckland

Prepared by Hamlyn Children's Books, an imprint of Reed Children's
Books Limited, Michelin House, 81 Fulham Road, London SW3 6RB,
and Auckland, Melbourne, Singapore and Toronto

ISBN 0-517-08769-3

Printed in China

Sally and Susie Bunny were twins, and it was their birthday. Their mother said they could have a small birthday party, with just a few friends.

They invited their uncle, Bert the Baker. Then they invited all the bunnies in their class. Then they invited all the brothers and sisters of all the bunnies in their class. Then they invited all the friends of all the bunnies they had already invited.

When the day came, hundreds of bunnies arrived.

Sally and Susie's mother was very angry. "This is ridiculous!" she said. "There won't be enough food to go around!"

The twins were horrified. They hadn't thought about food. All their guests looked very hungry.

Just at that moment, Bert arrived in his truck.

"I've got a surprise for you," he said, and he opened the truck doors. Inside was the biggest birthday cake they'd ever seen.

"Thanks!" they gasped. "You've saved the party!"

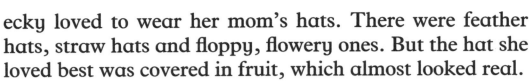

Becky loved to wear her mom's hats. There were feather hats, straw hats and floppy, flowery ones. But the hat she loved best was covered in fruit, which almost looked real.

But Mom did *not* like Becky wearing her hats at all, especially the fancy fruit one.

Then one day, while Mom was hanging out some wash on the clothesline, Becky put it on again. Next moment, she heard her mom cry "Oh, dear! No!"

Becky forgot she was wearing mom's hat and rushed out to see what was wrong. Suddenly, a gust of wind blew the hat clean off her head and into the air. It landed by the rose bed. As Becky rushed to catch it, she spotted something small and shiny.

"A ring!" gasped Becky.

"My *wedding* ring!" cried her mom. "My hands are wet, and it must have slipped off my finger. I might never have found it, but for you, Becky!"

Becky's mom was so pleased she gave her a very special present. So now Becky can wear her very *own* best, fancy fruit hat whenever she likes!

Sally was afraid of the dark. So each night her mother left her bedside lamp switched on.

"Come and look out of your bedroom window," said Sally's mother one evening. "I'm going to show you something special."

"I don't think I'll like it," said Sally. "It's nighttime, and it's dark out there."

Her mother smiled. "Come and see," she said, and she pulled the curtains open.

Sally gasped in surprise. There, in the sky over the field, floated a huge, silvery moon and billions of tiny, white stars. It was beautiful.

"Everyone has their own little star," said Sally's mother. "You can choose your star, Sally. Even when the clouds hide it, it will still be shining all night long for you. Just like your bedside lamp."

Sally snuggled under her comforter and thought about her star.

"I'm going to sleep now, mama," she said. "And I don't want my bedside lamp on. I'm not afraid of the dark now that I know my star is shining for me."

Terry liked to draw.

He drew on the walls and on the floor. He even climbed on top of the cupboard and drew on the ceiling. At school, he drew in all the reading books. He drew everywhere, all the time.

At last, his teacher had an idea.

"Terry," she said. "Let's paint a huge picture on the wall at the end of the playground. You can be in charge of the job, and the other bunnies in your class can help you. If we do that, will you promise to stop drawing everywhere, all the time, and do some other kinds of school work, just sometimes?"

Terry promised. The next day, he made a design for the big picture. The day after that, work on the wall began. And a week later, it was finished. Terry was very proud. It looked wonderful.

And Terry did *try* to keep his promise.

Four young bunnies wanted to go out and play.

"Wear your gloves—it's cold!" Mom told them.

So they took out a big pile of blue wool gloves from the closet, and pulled on the first ones they picked up.

"Mine are too small!" cried the first bunny.

"Mine are too big!" moaned the second bunny.

"Mine are uncomfortable!" said the third bunny.

"You've put on two right gloves!" laughed the fourth bunny.

"You're *all* wearing the wrong ones!" smiled Mom. "We had better go shopping!"

At the store, she bought four new pairs of gloves: yellow ones for the first bunny, red ones for the second bunny, a green pair for the third bunny, and brown for the fourth bunny.

"Your old gloves had holes in them, anyway," said Mom. "And you were always mixing them up!"

The next morning, the young bunnies wanted to go and play again. But not one of them could remember which color gloves were theirs.

Can you?

The Bunnies were walking home late one summer night. It was dark, and there was no moon.

Father Bunny switched on his flashlight, but the battery was dead, and it didn't work.

Father Bunny set off into the darkness, saying: "This way, kids!" and the young bunnies followed.

Mother Bunny said: "Are you sure this is the right way? It's too dark to see."

Father Bunny was cross. He said, "We should have set off earlier, while it was still light."

The little bunnies were frightened of getting lost. They were frightened of foxes, of cats and badgers, and wished they were at home.

Then they heard a tiny voice, down by their feet. It was Dora, the glowworm.

"Want a light? I can show you the way," said Dora.

"Thanks, Dora," said the bunnies, and they set off after her as she guided them safely, all the way home.

There was once a bunny who was such a crybaby, everyone called him Baby Bunny. If he fell over, he would cry, even when it didn't hurt. If the squirrels whizzed past on their skateboards, Baby Bunny cried, even though he saw them coming. The smallest thing would start him crying. He was the biggest crybaby around.

One day, Baby Bunny was in the yard blowing up a balloon to play with. But he couldn't tie a knot in it and was about to cry when, suddenly, he spotted a fox climbing into the window of the house next door. Baby Bunny knew his neighbors were out. Then the fox must be a burglar!

Poor Baby Bunny was so frightened, he let go of the balloon. It shot through the air making such a strange noise that it startled the fox, who fell from the window.

Baby Bunny's dad rushed outside and caught him.

"It was Baby Bunny who really caught me," admitted the fox.

"I d. . .did? I mean, I DID!" said Baby Bunny, feeling much braver. And, from that day on, he was called BRAVE Bunny, instead.

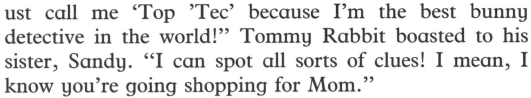

Just call me 'Top 'Tec' because I'm the best bunny detective in the world!" Tommy Rabbit boasted to his sister, Sandy. "I can spot all sorts of clues! I mean, I know you're going shopping for Mom."

"How?" asked Sandy.

"You're carrying her purse and shopping bag!"

"Anyone could have guessed that!" sniffed Sandy.

Later, Tommy saw Sandy in the kitchen. "You've been helping Mom with the cooking!" he said. "There's flour on your apron!"

"That was an easy clue to see!" replied Sandy, leaving the room. Tommy looked in the cabinet and found a box full of cakes with chocolate icing on them.

"There you are!" Sandy called to Tommy later. "I knew you'd eat one!"

"Eat what?" said Tommy.

"A chocolate cake!" said Sandy.

"How could you tell?" asked Tommy. "Fingerprints on the box?"

"No," smiled Sandy. "FOOTprints! You dropped some icing and stepped on it! You're tracking it everywhere!"

Tommy hurried to clean it up.

"*I'm* the top 'tec around here!" laughed Sandy.

Every morning, when Alexandra heard the mail drop into the mailbox, she rushed to see if there was anything for her. Most days, there wasn't.

"Just bills," sighed Dad. "Always bills."

"No one ever writes to me," said Alexandra. They don't even send me bills."

Then she had an idea. She wrote letters—to her granny, her grandfather, her aunts and uncles, her cousins, her big sister at college, her teacher, her best friend, and the mail carrier. She wrote a short letter to each one and drew a picture. Her mom helped her write the names and addresses on the envelopes. Then she mailed the letters.

Everyone wrote back. By the end of the week, Alexandra had a huge pile of letters.

"That's nice," she said. But then her mom reminded her, "Now you'll have to write back to everyone!"

"I don't mind," said Alexandra.

And she didn't.

Mike and Sally didn't want their vacation to end. They wanted to stay by the ocean forever.

When they got home, they were both cross.

"Let's go back on vacation," they said. "Let's not get out of the car."

"All right," said their mother. She left them in the car and went indoors.

After a while, they smelled supper cooking.

"We must stay here until they take us back to the beach," said Sally.

Through the living-room window, they could see their father turn on the television.

"We're not moving," said Mike.

"I wonder what's on television?" said Sally.

"I hope they leave us some supper," said Mike.

They watched their parents start eating.

"Look! French fries!" said Mike. "My favorite!" And he jumped out of the car and ran indoors.

"Wait for me!" called Sally, and ran in after him.

hoopee! Ride 'em, cowboy!" shouted Bronco Bunny, waving his stetson in the air. With his other paw, he clutched the reins of his horse, as it snorted and reared.

Bronco hung on as he bounced and bumped about. He was the king of the rodeo show—there wasn't another cowboy in the whole Wild West who could ride like Bronco Bunny.

And what a sight he looked, too. He wore a leather vest over his checked shirt, a polka dot scarf around his neck, and big, black boots. His belt had a large, shiny buckle at the front, shaped like cowhorns.

The crowd yelled excitedly as Bronco stayed in the saddle longer than any other rider. The horse did all it could to throw him. But Bronco was not to be beaten. Until . . .

Suddenly, he fell with a thud!

"What was that noise?" asked Mrs. Bunny, hurrying into the room.

"I fell off my horse," groaned Bronco.

"You mean my sofa!" frowned his mum.

"Sorry," said Bronco. "Anyway, I won't play cowboys again. It hurts!"

Rob and Rita Rabbit had a date. So Rob put on his new jacket to make sure he looked his best. When he stopped to get Rita, she had dressed up, too. "I'll take you to the 'Bunnies' Burger Bar,'" said Rob. "It has just opened. It's a great place to go and eat!"

"That's very kind of you," replied Rita. "But I'm not very hungry."

Rob told her all about the delicious, big bumper burgers and ice cream desserts that were served there.

"M'mm!" said Rita, licking her lips. "I'm hungry now!" she smiled. So they both hurried into town on their roller skates.

"Hurry up, slowpoke," called Rita, who led the way. "I can't wait!"

"Oh, no! I'm afraid you'll have to," sighed Rob, as they stopped in the middle of the shopping center. "See?" he added, pointing to the burger bar. "It's shut today! Just our luck! What shall we do now?"

"Race you back home for a tasty carrot and lettuce sandwich," smiled Rita, as she set off again down the main street.

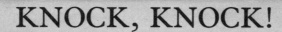
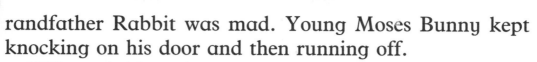
Grandfather Rabbit was mad. Young Moses Bunny kept knocking on his door and then running off.

"I'll teach him a lesson," thought Grandfather Rabbit. He put on a fox mask and hid behind the door.

As soon as the young bunny knocked, Grandfather Rabbit jumped out, shouting "Grrrrr!"

Moses was too scared to run away. He burst into tears. Grandfather Rabbit took off his mask.

"I'm sorry. I didn't mean to upset you," he said. "But I'm getting fed up. I can't watch the television in peace."

Moses said he was sorry, too. He promised not to play tricks again.

"Good," said Grandfather Rabbit. Then he said, "Would you like the mask?"

"Yes, please!" said little Moses. And he put the mask on and ran home, shouting "GRRR! GRRRRR! GRRRRRRRR!" all the way.

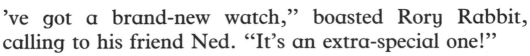
I've got a brand-new watch," boasted Rory Rabbit, calling to his friend Ned. "It's an extra-special one!"

"Why?" asked Ned.

"It tells the date!" replied Rory, proudly.

Rory asked Ned to show him the basement.

"What for?" said Ned.

"You'll soon see!" replied Rory, mysteriously. So Ned got a flashlight and led the way.

"Turn off your flashlight just for a minute," Rory told Ned, who didn't really want to.

"See?" Rory said, pointing to his watch. "It even glows in the dark!"

Ned was pleased when they had left the basement.

"Can we go in the backyard now?" asked Rory.

"Do you want to play football, then?" said Ned, eagerly.

"Oh, no, said Rory. "I want to show you something else about my watch."

Outside, he took the watch off his wrist and dipped it in the shallow pond. "It's waterproof, too!" he grinned.

"Does it keep good time?" asked Ned.

Rory looked and suddenly ran off.

"Yes, it does!" he called. "And I'm fifteen minutes and ten seconds late for lunch!"

Penny hated rain. She wouldn't go outside in it. She thought it would flatten her fur. Ugh! And besides she could never think of any games she wanted to play in the rain.

Today it was raining. So Penny sat and moped all morning.

After lunch it was still raining. Penny sat and stared out at the gray clouds. Then who should she see but her friends, Mo and Robin. And there was Kate, and Shawn, and Susie. They were playing "Jump the Puddle." Then Shawn took a toy boat out of his pocket. He floated it on a puddle. Robin made waves for it. The others laughed. They were having fun.

Penny watched. "I suppose I could *try* going out in the rain," she said to her mother.

She put on her shiny red raincoat and her boots. She tied her hood on carefully. She stepped outside. She didn't get wet. "Hello, Penny, come and play 'Cross the River,'" said Mo. And Penny had a lovely time. "I think I like rain, Mo," she said.

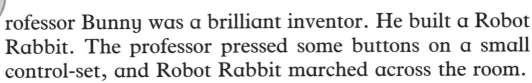

Professor Bunny was a brilliant inventor. He built a Robot Rabbit. The professor pressed some buttons on a small control-set, and Robot Rabbit marched across the room.

"It can do anything!" the professor explained to all the bunnies who came to see his invention.

The professor pushed more buttons, and Robot Rabbit dug the garden, cut the grass, painted the front door, made sandwiches, fetched and carried, and even washed the dishes and cups. And that was only the start!

"It can talk, too!" the professor proudly told his visitors.

"I A-M A R-O-B-O-T!" said Robot Rabbit in a strange, crackly voice.

"Can it hop?" asked a young rabbit. The professor thought hard for a moment, before using the controls again.

Suddenly, Robot Rabbit jumped about. Some pieces dropped off it. The robot stopped, swayed to and fro, then fell over with a bang!

"No, it can't!" replied the professor. "I never thought of that!"

"But *all* bunnies hop!" smiled the young rabbit.

"Robot Rabbit will, too, when I mend it!" the professor laughed.

Emily's birthday was very soon. She knew exactly what she wanted. She wanted wings.

She wanted to fly high above the countryside and watch the other bunnies, far below.

But when she told her mother and father, they just laughed and said, "Bunnies belong on the ground."

On the morning of her birthday, Emily woke up very early and found a note by her bed. It said, "In the garden, up the oak tree."

Emily crept outside and tiptoed toward the big oak tree. A yellow rope ladder was hanging down from one of the branches.

Emily climbed up and up until she reached a little tree house, painted green so it was hidden among the leaves. Inside was another note, which said: "Sorry we couldn't get wings, but we've made you a little house, high in the branches, instead. Bunnies don't really have to stay on the ground all the time! Love from Mom and Dad."

For a whole month before Christmas, the bunnies searched in all the closets and cupboards to see where their mother had hidden their presents.

By Christmas Eve, they still hadn't found them.

"Perhaps she hasn't bought any presents," said Susie, the eldest. "She said money was a bit short. I bet Santa Claus forgets us, too."

But they hung up their stockings and then, sadly, went to bed. They were sure Christmas was going to be a disappointment.

But, when morning came, they had a surprise. There were plenty of presents, big packages and little parcels from their mom and their grannies and from all their uncles and aunts, and stockings full of gifts from Santa. And there was a message from their mom, too. It said:

"Merry Christmas! Don't you think a surprise is fun? I do! You'll never guess where I hid your presents—and I'm not going to tell you. I want to use the same place next year. Love, Mom."

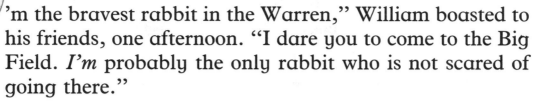

I'm the bravest rabbit in the Warren," William boasted to his friends, one afternoon. "I dare you to come to the Big Field. *I'm* probably the only rabbit who is not scared of going there."

Now, all the little rabbits were forbidden to visit the Big Field. "There are owls and foxes there," they said. "You mustn't go, William." It's very scary, and you might get hurt.

"Pooh," said William, rudely. "I'll explore it by myself then." And off he went.

At last, William reached the Big Field. He stopped. It was already getting dark, and everything was very still. William felt a bit scared. Suddenly he heard a long, low hoot. It was an owl. That *really* frightened William. He raced to a hedge, squeezed through, and ran and ran. Then he heard a shout, and there was a little light bobbing across the field. It was his father, looking for him with a flashlight.

William ran to his dad. "I was very very frightened," he said. His dad hugged William tightly. "Don't ever go off alone again," he said. "I won't," promised William, and he snuggled safely in his father's arms as they began the long walk home.

One rainy afternoon, Rob and Rita Rabbit were watching television with their friends when the news came on. One of the news stories was all about a famous actor who had just made a film. The star was being interviewed outside a theater. Lots of fans were cheering and shouting at him.

"I wish **I** could be a movie star," sighed Rob, dreamily.

"We can pretend you are one," smiled Rita. "It would make a good game to play."

The others agreed. So they turned off the television and imagined that Rob was famous.

Rob pretended to be arriving for the opening of his own new film. The other rabbits cheered as he waved to them.

"Can we have your autograph, please?" they asked Rob.

"Of course!" he said, while they found some paper. Rob got a pencil and had to write down his name for each of his friends.

"I don't think I'd want to be a star, after all," he sighed, a little later. "All this writing makes my paw *ache*!"

Young Rosy Rabbit loved to wear very colorful clothes. When she put on her red ribbon, orange sweater, yellow scarf, green skirt, blue socks, and violet gloves, she looked as bright as a rainbow.

"My friends even call me Rainbow Rabbit!" Rosy told her mom, who was in the kitchen.

"Would you like to take them some of my home-baked cookies?" smiled Mom.

"M'mm! Yes, please!" said Rosy. She reached up and opened the cabinet door to find the cookie jar. But, suddenly, a big bag of flour dropped out, and flour fell all over her. Rosy disappeared in a dusty, white cloud.

"What a mess!" said Mom. "But no harm done!"

"Except I'm white all over," gasped Rosy, peering in a mirror. Sure enough, her clothes were white, her face was white, and even her long, furry ears were white.

"I'd better wash and change before I meet my friends now!" said Rosy.

"I wonder what they'd say if they saw you like that?" smiled Mom.

"They'd probably call me *White Wabbit*!" joked Rosy.

Builder Bunny was always building things. He built a red-brick barbecue for Silas Squirrel, a dollhouse for the Bunny Twins, a model boat for Felix Fox, and a tool shed for Digger Rabbit.

Builder was always busy and always thinking of the next thing he could build for someone.

"Perhaps it will be a new front door or even a whole house!" he chuckled, while he worked away happily.

In fact, it wasn't to be either of those things. For, next moment, Silas came to find him. "My new neighbor, Glenda Goose, needs something built right now!" he said.

"I'll be pleased to do it, whatever it is!" replied Builder, following his friend home. Silas soon introduced him to Glenda.

"I want a cabinet for my kitchen, please," she said. So Builder set to work.

"It's very kind of you," smiled Glenda, when Builder had finished. "Why on earth do you build so many things for everyone?"

"Simple!" laughed Builder. "Because, while I make things, I make *new friends*, too!"

Digger Rabbit enjoyed digging things up.

"Why do you do that?" asked a family of squirrels he met in the woods one day.

"I dig up very old things that belonged to people long ago!" Digger replied proudly. "Like old vases and pots," he added. "It's very important work. I've dug up all sorts of bits and pieces. They are in the museum now, for everyone to see!"

The squirrels thought he was very clever.

"Well, I must be on my way," said Digger. "I am very busy!"

"So are we!" replied the squirrels.

Next morning, in the woods, they were surprised to see holes all over the ground. Just then, they spotted Digger digging away.

"Hello!" he called. "I decided to dig here today for old things. But the only things I've dug up all day are nuts and acorns."

"They are our winter food store," replied the squirrels.

"Oh, sorry," smiled Digger. "I'll put them back."

"Then for once you'll be *burying* things!" they giggled.

Fran and Trish had decided to have a midnight snack. Together the two little bunnies smuggled cakes and fruit into their room and hid them under their quilts. That night, as soon as the burrow was quiet, Fran whispered, "Are you awake, Trish?" Trish sat up. "Is it time for our snack yet?" she yawned.

Just then, there was bright flash of lightning and a great rumble of thunder. "I'm scared," said Fran, diving under the covers.

Their mother opened the door. "Good gracious, what are you doing?" she said.

"We were going to have a midnight snack, Mom, but the storm scared us," said Trish. "And I've sat on at least one of the cakes."

"You naughty girls," scolded their mother. "You should be fast asleep. But since there's a storm, I'll stay with you a while. Eat your snack now, and then brush your teeth. But you can help me change the sheets first, young lady," she said to Trish.

So they ate their snack while the thunder crashed around them. And luckily they were forgiven for making such a mess.

Joe's dad had a tent. It was a small tent, and it was old, but it was strong and it kept out the wind and the rain.

"Can I sleep in the tent tonight, dad?" asked Joe one summer day.

"Yes, why not," said his dad, and that afternoon they put the tent up together. Joe got his flashlight and his sleeping bag. He took a pillow and his favorite comic book. His mom made him some sandwiches and a thermos of hot milk. He was ready.

For once, Joe wanted it to be bedtime. He crawled into the tent. The flashlight made huge shadows on its sides. Joe could hear an owl hooting. But he wasn't scared. It felt cozy inside the tent. He looked out of the flap and saw the stars twinkling.

I'd like to live in a tent forever, thought Joe as he snuggled inside his sleeping bag.

And do you know, Joe grew up to be a famous explorer. And he took the old tent all over the world with him on all his exciting adventures.

Cliff wanted to see who was best at jumping.

"I can jump highest," said Cliff.

"But I'm taller," replied his friend. Paul had longer legs, but they were not as strong.

"I'm the best," said Cliff. "We'll see," said Paul.

"Let's see if we can jump onto that," said Cliff pointing to a bird feeder. "Okay," replied Paul doubtfully. It looked very high. But he couldn't change his mind now.

Paul went first. "One. Two. Three. Go," said Cliff. Paul ran very fast. "Whee," he shouted as he jumped. He landed safely. "Phew," he said to himself with relief as he climbed back down.

"Right. My turn," said Cliff. "This will be easy." Cliff ran fast. He jumped so high he nearly went right over the bird feeder. He just managed to hold onto the edge. "Help. Help, I'm stuck!" he shouted.

Paul thought quickly. He gathered up lots of grass and put it under the bird feeder. Cliff dropped onto the soft grass.

"That's the last jumping competition we're going to have," said Cliff.

"Thank goodness for that," thought Paul.

Ellen and her friends liked playing in Farmer Smith's junk pile. One day, they found a rusty bucket and an old boot.

They were just looking inside the bucket when Ellen heard a noise. She looked around and saw a family of field mice carrying suitcases.

"Hello," said Ellen. "Hello," said one of the mice sadly. Ellen asked what was wrong. "We haven't got a home," said the biggest mouse. "We used to live in the hay field, but all the hay's been cut. It'll be winter soon. Do you know anywhere warm that we can live?"

Everyone thought hard, but nobody could help. The poor mice said goodbye and walked sadly away.

Ellen and her friends went back to the junk pile. But they couldn't play because they were so sad.

Then Ellen had an idea. "This old boot will make a lovely home," she said. "We'll mend the holes and paint it. And then we'll put lots of straw inside. The mice will keep warm all winter."

The mice were so delighted with their new home they invited everyone to a party.

Donna had a new baby sister. Mother had just brought her home from the hospital. Donna thought she was lovely.

The new baby didn't yet have a name. Donna wanted to call her Fluffy, but mother thought it would be too old-fashioned. Father liked Stella, but nobody else did. So the new baby went without a name.

One day, Donna and her mother were baking a cake, while the baby slept peacefully in her crib.

Suddenly they heard an odd noise. Donna looked around and saw that baby was standing on top of the crib trying to reach a carrot. Before mother could do anything, Baby began to topple, and over she went.

Donna closed her eyes and waited for the bang. But nothing happened. Baby had fallen into the clothes basket and was laughing.

Donna said to Mother, "I've got a good name for baby. We should call her 'Lucky.'" Mother thought for a minute. "Yes," she said, "that's a very good name."

Andrew was very excited because it was Christmas Eve. He wanted to see Santa Claus, but he knew Santa would only come when he was asleep.

Andrew tried his best to sleep. He closed his eyes tight. But try as he might, he just could not get to sleep. After a long time, he opened an eye. He could just make out his stocking in the dark at the end of the bed. No. Santa Claus hadn't come. It was still empty.

Andrew got out of bed and put all his toys away. He didn't want Santa to fall over anything. Then he folded his clothes neatly on a chair.

At last Andrew felt tired. But he decided to listen at the door before getting into bed. He couldn't hear anything, but he hoped Santa hadn't forgotten about him. Before long, Andrew was fast asleep.

Santa Claus always comes down the chimney to bring his presents. It is a very good thing, too, because Andrew had fallen asleep next to the door. Nobody else could have gotten into his bedroom that night.

I

t was raining. Big, dribbly drops of water plopped and splashed on the field. Liz, Ann and Janie moped in their burrow. Janie was especially sad. She liked playing outdoors best.

"You could dress up," said their mother. "Go and look in the big box in our room, and see what you can find."

The girls rushed off to their parents' room. There was a big box in the corner. It was full of dresses and big, knobbly shoes, and soft hats and shiny bracelets.

Liz squealed with excitement. "I'm going to be a princess," she said. "*I'm* going to dress up like Mama at her wedding," said Ann.

Janie didn't know what she wanted to be. Then she saw something right at the bottom of the box. It was a huge, yellow raincoat, with long sleeves and a shiny yellow hat to match. "I'm going to be a fisherman," she laughed. "And I can play outside and stay as dry as a bone!"

So off she went. She didn't get wet, and she made the biggest mud pie you have *ever* seen.

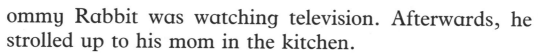
Tommy Rabbit was watching television. Afterwards, he strolled up to his mom in the kitchen.

"Howdy, ma! Figure I'll ride on into town!" "You won't," replied Mom. "Why are you talking like that?"

"Tex does!" said Tommy.

"Who's he?" asked Mom, puzzled.

"The sheriff on TV," said Tommy. "I love cowboy movies!"

Tommy kept talking like Tex until he went to bed.

Next day, Tommy watched another film.

"Ahoy, me hearties! Avast and belay!" he called out.

"What do you mean?" they asked.

"It's pirate talk, like Captain Brassbutton speaks on TV."

Tommy pretended to be Captain Brassbutton all day.

The next afternoon, Mom saw there was a really old film on the television. "Look, Tommy!" she called.

When it had finished, Tommy didn't say a word for a whole hour.

"He's copying the hero in that film!" Mom smiled at Dad. "I love *silent movies* best!"

Tommy Rabbit was doing a jigsaw puzzle. "It will take me ages!" he thought.

But Tommy didn't mind. He liked puzzles. Soon Brian Bunny called to him. "Coming out to play?" Brian asked.

"No, thanks," replied Tommy. "I'm enjoying my puzzle!"

"H'm!" muttered Brian, thoughtfully picking up some pieces of it. "This bit goes there, and that piece fits here!"

While Brian put in another piece, there was a knock at the door. It was Bruce Bunny. "Hello, Tommy! Let's go out and play!" said Bruce.

"But I want to do my puzzle!" replied Tommy. So did Bruce. "I'm good at those! Let me try!" he grinned.

Then the Bunny Twins arrived. "Let's play ball in the park, Tommy!" they said. But they saw everyone around the jigsaw puzzle and joined in, too.

Finally, there was another knock on the door.

"It's a great day to play outside, Tommy!" said Maurice Mouse.

"I can't," replied Tommy. "I'm busy doing a puzzle!"

"Not any more!" called the others. "We've finished it!"

So Tommy went out to play, after all!

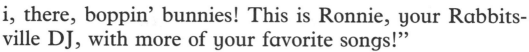

Hi, there, boppin' bunnies! This is Ronnie, your Rabbitsville DJ, with more of your favorite songs!"

Ronnie was at the radio station, presenting his morning music program. It was very successful. But being a disk jockey was hard work!

Ronnie always had to be at the studio extra early, to pick the top songs to play. During the show, rabbits would phone in their record requests, too. So Ronnie spent all his spare time keeping up with the latest sounds.

There wasn't a song he hadn't heard, a record he hadn't played. When he wasn't "on the air," he spent hours tuned in to other radio music shows, to be sure his was different.

"It's about time you had a vacation," said Ronnie's boss, one day.

"I do need a rest," agreed Ronnie. So, after announcing to his fans he would be back in a week, Ronnie flew off . . . to a distant, desert island.

"The perfect place!" he smiled, sitting on the beach and listening to the sound of the surf.

"Not a single radio around!"

Jenny and Alison were best friends. They did everything together. Then Alison's family moved to another burrow, several fields away. Jenny was lonely. "I miss Alison," she said to her mother.

"Why don't you write her a letter," said Jenny's mom. "Tell her about school and about visiting Granny last weekend. I've got some pretty paper. You can write your letter on that."

So Jenny sat at the table and wrote her letter. She finished it, "Lots of love from Jenny." She put a stamp on the envelope and mailed it at the Warren Post Office.

Each day, Jenny thought of more things to tell her friend. She started a new letter and wrote a little bit every day. Then one morning, there was a letter for her. "It's from Alison," said Jenny. "She misses me, too, and she's sent me a photo."

"There you are," said Jenny's mom. "You may be a long way away, but you can write to each other, and one day I expect you'll see each other again. Best friends are friends wherever they are."

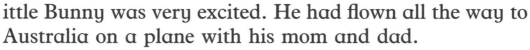

Little Bunny was very excited. He had flown all the way to Australia on a plane with his mom and dad.

"It's very kind of your Uncle Joe to invite us to stay with him in the bush!" said Dad.

Little Bunny was puzzled. "I thought he lived in a house, not a bush!" he said.

Dad laughed. He explained that the big, wild center of Australia, where Uncle Joe ran a sheep farm, was called the bush.

When they arrived, it was very hot. Little Bunny had never seen so many sheep before.

"How many do you have?" he asked Uncle Joe.

"Count them!" chuckled Uncle Joe.

As Little Bunny began, he suddenly saw the biggest, strangest rabbit, which bounded past him.

Little Bunny was very startled. He ran to tell his parents and Uncle Joe. "It's a giant rabbit!" he cried.

When they all went to look, Uncle Joe laughed. "That's not a rabbit, that's a kangaroo," he chuckled. "They hop around, like rabbits—but with giant jumps!"

"They should be called BUSH BUNNIES!" chuckled Little Bunny.

Peggy decided to run away to sea.

She took her bear, and her favorite book, and a piece of carrot cake, and set off.

She met Algernon the Mole.

"Which way is the sea?" she asked.

"I don't know," said Algernon.

She met Freda the fieldmouse. Freda didn't know, either, but she thought it was a long way away. Peggy asked everyone she met the way to the sea, but no one knew.

So Peggy sat down on a log, ate her carrot cake, and thought. She decided that maybe she wasn't quite old enough to leave home, and maybe she'd rather sleep in her own bed at night, than be out on the road, looking for the sea.

So she picked up her bear and her book, and headed back home.

Buster was the tallest rabbit in his class. But he didn't like being bigger than everyone else. He felt silly.

One day, there was a soccer game against another school. Everyone went to watch. Buster's class made a huge flag to wave. It said "GOOD LUCK, WARREN SCHOOL."

The field was crowded and the rabbits jostled for a good place to watch. Buster stood at the back where he could see over everyone's heads. Then someone stepped on the flag pole, which broke. Their flag was useless. The game started. It was exciting, but Warren School was losing. Suddenly Buster heard a snuffle beside him. It was little Tim. "I can't see," he squeaked. "Come on, Tim," said Buster. "You can sit on my shoulders, and I'll hold the flag up in my paws."

So Tim cheered, and Buster waved the flag, and suddenly Warren School scored a goal. And another. They had won!

The team captain shook Buster's paw and thanked the class for cheering the team on with the good-luck flag.

It's nice to be tall, after all, thought
Buster with a big smile.

Olivia was very excited. She was at a birthday party, and the magician was about to perform. Olivia really loved magicians and wanted to be one when she grew up.

The magician stood up in his brightly colored sparkly coat and top hat. "Boys and girls," he said. "I'm very sorry, but my assistant is not well, and so I will have to cancel today's show—unless . . . unless someone would care to volunteer to help."

All the rabbits shot their paws in the air. Eventually, he chose . . . Olivia! She almost fainted with excitement as she got up to take her place beside him. First she had to choose a card; then she had to pull swirling ribbons out of his pocket. Then she had to wave a magic wand over his top hat, which miraculously became full of handker-chiefs. The climax of the show was the magician sawing Olivia in half (of course, he didn't really, it was just a trick). The audience gasped. How *brave* Olivia was—yet there she was, still in one piece. Olivia and the magician bowed, and the audience clapped and cheered.

"When you graduate, would you like to be my assistant full time, Olivia?" asked the magician.

"Yes, I would," said Olivia. "But even more than that, I'd like to be a real magician!"

Buster Bunny was always busting things. That's why everyone called him Buster. It wasn't that he meant to break things. It just seemed to happen because Buster was a bit clumsy.

He broke Basil Bunny's best model airplane when he tried to fly it. Then he borrowed Rodney Rabbit's tennis racquet and broke that, too. Buster's closet was full of broken toys. He broke so many things that his mom put away her best china and refused to use it!

In the yard, Buster liked to help his dad dig up the weeds. But Buster broke the trowel and then overloaded the wheelbarrow and broke that, also!

"Busting things is no use to anyone at all!" Buster told Belinda Bunny, who lived down the road.

"Yes, it is!" she smiled. "Wait here!" She hurried home to get something.

"I'm going on vacation, tomorrow," said Belinda, when she returned. "All my savings are in this china piggy-bank. You're *just* the person to break it open for me!"

41

Georgia Rabbit was very excited. She was going to be the queen in the school play!

All the children in the class had been rehearsing for the play, and today they were going to try on their costumes. Georgia was given a very grand outfit. She would be wearing a long red dress with a gray train, red shoes, and a golden crown.

The day of the play arrived, and all the mothers and fathers arrived in the hall. In the middle of the play, Georgia realized that her crown was beginning to slip. Just as the king began to waltz her around the stage, Georgia's ears shot out from beneath the crown, which went rolling across the front of the stage.

Georgia was very upset—her first time on stage and she had spoiled it. Then she realized that the whole audience was smiling and clapping. She was a success! She did not try to find the crown. Instead, she became the first-ever queen with long, fluffy ears.

Bessie Bunny and her friend Maggie Mouse were going to a party. They both put on their best dresses and tied ribbons around their heads.

"I can't wait to get there!" squeaked Maggie, excitedly.

"Well, you can't go until you have brushed your teeth!" frowned her mother.

"Neither can you!" said Bessie's mom.

"That won't take long!" replied Maggie, hurrying upstairs to the bathroom. Sure enough, she was ready for a clean-teeth-inspection in no time.

"Very good!" smiled her mom. "Now you're all ready to go partying!"

"Where's Bessie?" asked Maggie, impatiently.

"Still in the bathroom!" replied Bessie's mother.

Five minutes passed, then fifteen, then half an hour. By now, Maggie Mouse was worried they would be late.

"Oh, do hurry up!" she called to Bessie Bunny.

At last, Bessie came out of the bathroom and showed her mother her huge, shining-white front teeth.

"What kept you?" asked Maggie, as they hurried away.

"My teeth take lots longer to clean," she told the mouse, "because they're so much **BIGGER** than yours!"

Bruce Bunny got a book of magic tricks for his birthday. He tried them out on his friend Bill Bunny. First, Bruce tied magic knots in a piece of string, then made them vanish! Next, he made a carrot appear as if from nowhere, and then he did all sorts of clever card tricks.

"Can you make a cookie vanish, too?" asked Bill.

Bruce nodded.

"So can I!" said Bill. He asked his mom for two small cookies and gave one to Bruce.

"Watch carefully," said Bruce, hiding the cookie in his paw. Then he put both paws behind his back, before holding them out, clenched, in front of him.

"The cookie is in your left paw!" said Bill. But he was wrong.

"I mean, your right paw!" added Bill. But he was wrong again. The cookie was nowhere to be seen!

"Now it's my turn," grinned Bill.

"You'll never do it!" frowned Bruce.

"Yes, I will! It's simple!" replied Bill. He popped the cookie in his mouth and ate it.

"Presto!" he chuckled. "All gone!"

All the young rabbits were out in the snow building snow bunnies. Mr. and Mrs. Fluff had announced that the best snow bunny would get a prize.

Andrea and Nicola were working hard on their snow bunny, but its ears kept breaking off, and they couldn't get the shape of its body right. "Call that a bunny? Looks more like a tortoise to me," jeered one of the boys.

Suddenly, Andrea had an idea. She whispered it to Nicola, and soon they'd made a plan.

It was time for the judging. Mr. and Mrs. Fluff looked Andrea's bunny up and down. They were impressed! It was exactly the right shape to be a real bunny, and my, what magnificent ears! And that tail looked just like the real thing. And as for the whiskers . . . They'd never seen such a likeness.

"Hang on, there's something fishy here," said Mr. Fluff. "You can't make whiskers out of snow."

"And—do I hear laughing?" asked Mrs. Fluff. "Surely snow bunnies don't laugh?"

So their secret was up. Nicola gave a great big shake, and the snow fell off. *She* had been the snow bunny! Everyone laughed. Although Andrea and Nicola didn't get a prize, Mr. and Mrs. Fluff gave them each a piece of chocolate for making them laugh.

Can I borrow a book, please?" Young Bunny asked Older Bunny, who kept lots and lots of them in his house. One room even had bookshelves on every wall.

"Of course!" said Older Bunny. "What sort of book would you like?"

"A big one," replied Young Bunny.

So Older Bunny got down a large book and gave it to him.

"Thank you," said Young Bunny, running home, next door. But, moments later, he brought the book back.

"Can I change it for a bigger book, please?" he asked.

Older Bunny was very puzzled. He went to find the biggest, thickest book he had. It was almost too heavy for Young Bunny to lift, so Older Bunny carried it for him.

"It's a very large book for a small bunny," said Older Bunny.

"It's just right!" said Young Bunny, who put it on the kitchen floor and carefully stood on it.

"See? Now I can reach the cookies on that shelf!"

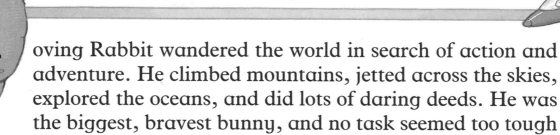

ROVING RABBIT

Roving Rabbit wandered the world in search of action and adventure. He climbed mountains, jetted across the skies, explored the oceans, and did lots of daring deeds. He was the biggest, bravest bunny, and no task seemed too tough for him!

He drove racing cars for a hobby and spent his vacations trekking through desert or deepest jungle.

Roving Rabbit was everyone's hero!

One day, as he returned home after another exciting expedition, Roving Rabbit had a visit from a top television host.

"I have a very special job for you," said the host.

"Name it!" said Roving Rabbit boldly. "Is it a spaceship to fly or ancient treasure to find?"

"Er. . .no," replied the host. "It's the chance to appear on my TV show — before your millions of fans! Just think of it!"

For a moment, Roving Rabbit did. Then he turned quite pale.

"Well, what do you say?" asked the host, eagerly. "Will you do it?"

"Thanks, but I couldn't," replied Roving Rabbit. "I'm much too *shy!*"

Arnold Rabbit, the famous rose grower, wanted to grow blue roses. But try as he might, he had no success.

He mentioned this to his brother Sinbad, who was a sailor and did not visit very often.

"No problem!" said Sinbad. "I can get you a blue rose plant. I picked one up on my travels."

The next day, Sinbad came by with a rose bush. It had beautiful dark blue flowers, and a lovely scent.

Arnold was delighted. He planted it next to the walk, in the front of his house. Then he said goodbye to Sinbad, who was going back to sea that very afternoon.

That night, it rained very hard. In the morning, Arnold went to look at the new rose.

"Goodness!" he said. "It's turned white!" It had. And there were big splashes of blue paint on the path.

Arnold took a deep breath and then laughed. "Just wait till that Sinbad gets back from his voyage!" he said. "I'll give him blue roses!"

Marjorie was late for school again. All the other bunnies were nearly at the gate, and Marjorie had to run all the way. Soon she was completely out of breath, and she had to sit down on a grassy bank.

Up above, in the blue sky, a lark was singing. It came down slowly and landed at Marjorie's feet. "Late again, Marjorie?" asked the lark.

"How do you know my name?" asked Marjorie.

"Every morning," said the lark, "I hear your friends calling you. Why are you always late?"

"Because I can't wake up early," said Marjorie.

"That's a funny sort of problem," said the lark. It's not one I've ever had." She thought for a while and then said, "Tell you what, I'll sing outside your window every day. I'll sing and sing, until you are up and dressed. Would that help?"

"Oh, yes, thank you, Mrs. Lark," said Marjorie. And that's what happened. And although Marjorie was very late for school that day, she was never late again.

Tommy Rabbit was playing the trumpet. Or, rather, he was trying to!

"It's not very easy to learn," he turned to his sister, Sandy, who finally took her paws away from her ears.

"I wish you'd hurry up!" she replied.

"I don't think I want to, after all!" said Tommy. He ran around to Brian Bunny's house to return the trumpet he had borrowed.

Later, Tommy came back with a drum. Rat-a-ta-thud! Ker-bang! Now the noise was worse than ever as he practiced on it.

"I met Bruce Bunny," Tommy told Sandy. "He said I could use his drum for as long as I wanted to!"

"Another minute would be too long!" she frowned, covering her ears again.

"I don't think I'll make a good drummer, either," sighed Tommy later. "But what can I play?"

His sister fetched a little box and gave it to him. When Tommy lifted the lid, he heard a tune.

"You can play my new *MUSIC BOX*," smiled Sandy.

"I agree it sounds much better!" laughed Tommy.

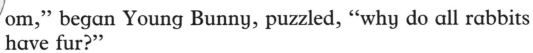

"**M**om," began Young Bunny, puzzled, "why do all rabbits have fur?"

"We'd look funny without it!" She smiled as she looked around from making the bed.

Young Bunny had just hurried in from the backyard, where he had seen a bird preening itself.

"But why don't we have feathers, like birds do?" asked Young Bunny.

"We'd look even funnier then!" laughed Mom. "Now be a good bunny and get me that pillow, please."

Young Bunny was still deep in thought. As he picked up the pillow, it got caught in the bed frame. Young Bunny gave the pillow a tug. There was a ripping noise, and feathers flew out everywhere!

Lots landed all over him. Some tickled his nose and made him sneeze! Others got caught under his sweater.

"It's not really funny!" said Mom, as Young Bunny began to laugh and laugh till the tears rolled down his laughing face.

"I can't help it!" replied Young Bunny, removing his sweater to free the feathers. "Now I know why bunnies have fur. Feathers really *tickle*!"

Ben was a forgetful little rabbit.

He forgot to brush his teeth.

He forgot to put his toys away.

He even forgot he'd left his favorite dump truck outside until his brother brought it in, all wet and rusty from the rain.

One morning, Ben's best friend Tim invited him to a family picnic at the beach. "I'll pack your lunch," said his mother. "Go and get your bathing suit, Ben."

Ben had forgotten where to find his swimsuit, but he looked in every drawer in the burrow until he found it. He put it on the kitchen table. "We're ready," said Tim. "'Bye, Mom," said Ben, and he grabbed his lunch box and ran out of the burrow.

After lunch and games at the beach, Tim's dad dipped a paw in the water. "It's lovely and warm," he said. "Let's swim."

But, oh, dear, where was Ben's bathing suit? "I left it on the kitchen table," he wailed.

So Ben sat on the beach feeling sorry for himself, while Tim's family played and swam in the water.

"I'll never forget anything again," said Ben.

And he never did.

THE DAY GARY MOVED

he Smith rabbits were moving. Everything was packed and ready. Everyone was excited. Except for Gary. He didn't want to move. He liked their damp, drafty burrow. He liked the hole in the wall where his books and his toy tractor just fit. And he liked to look outside and see the brown tree trunk nearby.

"Come on, Gary. It's time to go," called his father.

"I'm not coming," said Gary. "I'm staying here."

Gary's dad had to pick him up and carry him all the way to the new burrow, while Gary sobbed on his shoulder.

"You'll like it, son, really you will," said his dad.

"I won't," snuffled Gary. "It won't be the same."

It wasn't the same. The Smiths' new burrow was dry and warm. Gary had a room of his very own, with lots of space for books and toys. And on the first morning after they arrived, he woke up and saw more brown tree trunks than he could count. And grass, shining in the sun.

Gary smiled. "I won't forget our old home," he thought. "But I *do* like this one."

Annie liked bedtime. She put her dolls in a row on her pillow.

"Get ready to go to sleep," she said to each doll. Then she told them a story. It was nearly always a short story, but that was all right, because the dolls were small and were soon asleep.

Then it was Annie's turn to get ready. She brushed her teeth with her yellow toothbrush.

"My teeth are all white and clean," she said to her reflection in the bathroom mirror.

Her mother brushed Annie's fur until all the snags and snarls were smoothed out and her coat shone like silk. Annie liked that.

Then she climbed into her pajamas. Sometimes she put her left paw in the right sleeve and her right paw in the left sleeve. Annie giggled when she saw she was all back to front.

At last, she jumped into bed. And then her mother read her a story. Annie liked that best of all. It was nearly always a short story, but that was all right because Annie was small. And — I expect you've guessed — she was soon fast asleep.

Ferdie was miserable, because he was no good at sports. All his friends could run and jump better than he could, and some could swim, too.

"I'm no good at anything," said Ferdie.

"Never mind," said his mom.

Sports Day was dreadful. Ferdie didn't win anything, and he often came last. To cheer himself up, he made a book about Sports Day.

He drew pictures of everyone, running, jumping, swimming and having a wonderful time. He drew himself, looking a bit sad. Then he wrote a story about Sports Day, and put it in his book.

His teacher said, "Well, Ferdie, you didn't win any races, but you've made the best book about Sports Day I've ever seen."

Ferdie was very proud. He took the book home.

"See?" he said. "I *am* good at something!"

"Of course you are," said his mother.

And she gave him a big hug.

LEO'S LETTUCE GARDEN

Leo loved food. He loved to eat juicy, orange carrots. He loved to eat round green peas that went "pop" out of their pods. But best of all, Leo loved to eat crisp, curly lettuce.

One day, Leo's father called him.

"Look, Leo," he said. "I've made a garden for you."

Leo looked. There was a square of freshly dug earth, and beside it was a small green watering can, a trowel, and a pack of seeds.

"Now you can grow your very own lettuce, Leo," said his father. "Dig a little trench, sow the seeds, and water them. If you look after them properly, they will grow into big, fat heads."

So Leo dug a trench and sowed the seeds one by one. He watered the earth every day, and soon the baby lettuce started to grow.

That summer, Leo had so much lettuce that he decided to give a lettuce party for all his friends. He gave each rabbit a big, crisp head of lettuce. "I grew them myself," he said proudly.

And everyone agreed it was the best lettuce they had ever eaten.

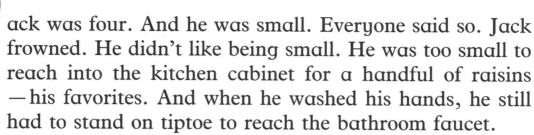

Jack was four. And he was small. Everyone said so. Jack frowned. He didn't like being small. He was too small to reach into the kitchen cabinet for a handful of raisins —his favorites. And when he washed his hands, he still had to stand on tiptoe to reach the bathroom faucet.

"I *hate* being small, Mom," said Jack.

"Listen to me, Jack," she said. "You can tie your shoelaces, can't you?"

"Yes," said Jack.

"You can use a knife and fork at mealtimes, can't you?"

"Yes," said Jack.

"And you can read, and count to twenty, and paint a picture?"

"Yes, I can," said Jack.

"Well," said his mom, "think of all those things you can do. Being big is learning to do lots of things by yourself —just like grownups.

Jack thought. "I *can* do lots of things," he said. "And I'm going to learn something else today, and tomorrow, and the next day. Four *is* big, after all."

illy had a sandbox in her garden. Everyone came to play in it. It was so big that you could roll over three times in it. You could build sand castles. And you could dig holes to bury treasure.

Then Jilly's friends stopped coming to the sandbox. "We're bored," they said. "We can't think of anything new to do in your sandbox, Jilly."

Jilly thought they were silly. "Come on," she said. "Let's build castles again." But no one wanted to.

Suddenly Jilly had a good idea. "We're rabbits, aren't we," she said. "And rabbits have long, strong back legs. Why don't we all get together and have a long jump contest?"

Jilly's friends thought this was a great idea. "We can have teams," said Jilly. "We'll see which team can jump the farthest. Anyone under eight can be in a team."

Soon all the young rabbits in the warren were in a team. Jilly was Long Jump Captain. They all learned to run fast and jump far.

"Even the fastest fox won't be able to catch us now," said Jilly's friends. "Thanks to Jilly's sandbox."

Gary's favorite toy was his dump truck. He called it Big Harry. It was bright yellow and had fat black wheels. Gary built mounds of earth and made Big Harry crawl up to the top and down the other side. He made Big Harry's engine noise. Vrrooom, Vrrooomm.

Gary was good at sharing his toys. He let Sam play with Big Harry. He helped old Mr. Johnson dig a new burrow, with Big Harry carrying the earth.

One day when Gary and Sam were playing, Sam fell over, right on top of Big Harry. Sam got up. He wasn't hurt. But Big Harry wouldn't move. It was broken. Gary burst into tears. "You broke it," he yelled at Sam. "Mom, Sam's broken Big Harry." Then Sam started to cry. "Listen," said Gary's mom. "It was an accident. Accidents sometimes happen. It wasn't Sam's fault. Big Harry isn't broken. You've just got dirt clogged in its wheels."

"Sorry, Sam," said Gary. "I'll play carefully now," said Sam. "Then there won't be any more accidents."

Cheri had two goldfish called Ebb and Flo.

Susie had a brown mouse. It could climb onto her head and nibble her ear. But Rachel didn't have a pet, and she wanted one more than anything else in the world.

"You'd have to feed and clean it," said Rachel's mother. "You do so many other things. When would you find time to look after a pet?"

One afternoon, Rachel found a box on the kitchen table. It said RACHEL on it in large letters. "Is it a pet?" asked Rachel. "Sort of," said her mother. "Look inside."

Rachel reached inside the box and took out something soft and furry. It had a beautiful snow-white coat and big, blue eyes. It looked like a baby rabbit.

"It's a glove puppet, Rachel," said her father. "Its name is Bunny. Put it over your paw, like this."

Rachel was thrilled. She could make her puppet move and cuddle it. She could carry it everywhere with her. And she didn't need to feed it or keep it clean.

"It's a *lovely* pet," she said. "Thank you, Mom. Thank you, Dad."

Mrs. Johnson was very old. Her legs were bent with age, and her fur was a nice shade of silvery white. She lived in a little thatched cottage at the edge of the woods, where she baked the most delicious cakes.

"Mrs. Johnson's silly," said Tom to his friends, Alice and Shawn. "She's not silly," said Alice. "She's just old. Mommy says she's very kind."

"She's not," said Tom. "She's silly."

One day, Mrs. Johnson gave each of the rabbits a slice of cake. "Thank you," said Alice and Shawn. "I don't want any," said Tom, rudely.

"Dear me, you're in a bad mood, young man," said Mrs. Johnson. "I'll tell you some jokes. Maybe they will cheer you up. What is a frog's favorite candy?" she said. "We don't know," giggled Alice. "A lollihop," said Mrs. Johnson.

Alice and Shawn laughed. Tom tried not to, but soon he was laughing, too.

"You see," said Alice, later. "Mrs. Johnson's not silly at all. You're the one that's silly, Tom."

Alice was right. And Tom never called Mrs. Johnson silly again.

It was Father's birthday. Rory and his mother were very pleased. They had bought Father a Rabbit Treadmill.

"This is just what Father needs. It will make him nice and slim again," said Mother.

"Yes," thought Rory. "Then I'll sit on his lap, and his stomach won't get in the way."

Mother went to the bakery to get Father's carrot top and cabbage birthday cake. "Now, don't play with the runner while I'm out," said Mother.

For a while, Rory played with his toys. But he soon got bored. "I wonder how the treadmill works," he thought. Rory pressed a big button on the handle. The machine made a whirring sound.

"I'll just have a little try," thought Rory. So he climbed on and started hopping. But the faster he hopped, the faster the machine went. Soon Rory was running so fast that he couldn't catch his breath.

Just then, Mother came home. "You do look thin and tired," she said. "Never mind. You can have some cake when Father gets home."

Good night," said Mother as she tucked Janet into bed. "Don't let the bedbugs bite."

"But I'm not sleepy," said Janet. "Oh dear," said mother. "Well, the best way to get to sleep is to count squirrels climbing trees. See if that works."

So Janet started counting. "One. Two. Three. Four . . . What comes after four?"

"Five," said a tiny voice. Janet looked around. Sitting on her pillow was a tiny squirrel. "Hello. My name's Helen," said the squirrel. "I'm bored with counting! Let's go and gather some acorns."

"But Mother won't let me go outside at night," said Janet.

"Don't worry. I'll look after you."

So they climbed out of the window and gathered lots of acorns. Then they put them in neat piles in Helen's store.

"I'm cold," said Janet, shivering. "Okay. I'll take you home now," said Helen.

Janet said goodbye to Helen and climbed into bed. Just as she began counting squirrels again, she heard Mother.

"Wake up, Janet. It's late. Do you want corn nibbles or carrot flakes for breakfast?"

I name this ship the 'Bunnyboat!'" announced Young Bunny. "And I'm proud to be her captain!"

With a splash, the brand-new Bunnyboat slipped gracefully into the water.

"Raise the mainsail!" yelled Young Bunny. "We're bound for the open sea!"

As the Bunnyboat sped along, Young Bunny called again. "There's a storm coming! All hands on deck!"

In no time, huge waves broke across the vessel's bow, sending spray flying. The Bunnyboat dipped, then rose again, threatening to capsize.

"Lower the sail and drop anchor!" shouted Young Bunny. "We'll ride out the storm yet, shipmates!"

Next moment, a familiar voice interrupted him. It was his mother, bringing a big towel.

"Just look!" she frowned. "You've splashed water all over the bathroom floor!"

"Sorry, Mom!" said Young Bunny. "I didn't mean to . . ."

"That's the last time I let you play with your toy boat in the bath," said Mom, "unless you promise not to splash everywhere!"

"Aye, aye, Mom!" said Young Bunny, getting out.

DREAMER

Last night, I dreamed I lived on a magic cloud which carried me to Lettuce Island!" Dreamer Bunny told his two friends.

"You always have great dreams!" they said.

Next day, Dreamer was fast asleep in a hammock in the backyard, when his friends called.

"I've just dreamed I was zooming through outer space in a carrot-shaped rocket!" said Dreamer, waking up.

"Want to see what we're doing, this afternoon?" his friends asked.

"I'm . . . ho, hum! . . . too sleepy," replied Dreamer with a yawn. So they left him to doze again.

When Dreamer opened his eyes at last, he saw a rabbit knight walking toward the gate. Beside him was a rabbit with big white wings!

"Wow!" gasped Dreamer, in amazement. "I must still be dreaming!"

"No, you're not!" called a familiar voice. "It's us!"

Dreamer stared hard and saw it was his two friends in home made costumes.

"We're putting on a play. We thought you might like to watch it now," they said.

"I wouldn't *DREAM* of missing it!" laughed Dreamer.

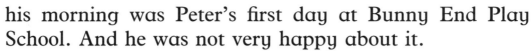

This morning was Peter's first day at Bunny End Play School. And he was not very happy about it.

"Do I have to go to school today?" he asked.

"Yes. You'll like it when you get there," said Father.

"But I want to play on my new bike," said Peter.

"Well," replied Father, "they may have one at school."

So they walked to Peter's new school. "Don't go," said Peter. So his father agreed to stay for a while.

Peter was very shy at first. He watched the others playing games. Then the teacher asked if he would like to do some pasting.

"Okay," said Peter. So he made a picture of his new bike with colored paper and glue. He didn't notice when his father left.

Everyone then sat in a circle. They had a carrot and a drink. Then they sang some songs. Afterwards, the teacher read them a story.

Soon Peter's father came to pick him up. "I like it here," said Peter. "Can I go to school forever?"

Yippee, it's my birthday," said James as he woke up. He raced downstairs.

"Happy birthday," said Mother as James ran past. "Do I have lots of presents?" asked James.

"Wait and see," said Mother.

"Am I going to have a party?"

"Wait and see," said Father.

"Will all my friends be there?"

"Wait and see," said Mother.

"Will I have a big cake with candles?"

"You'll have to wait and see," said Father. "But I can't wait," said James jumping about. "I'm too excited."

James went to find his friends. He asked if they knew about his party. No, nobody knew anything. So James went home to wait. He waited and waited.

Then Father called, "James, come here." James was so excited that his nose wouldn't stop twitching.

"Get your coat on," said Father. "We're going out."

"Oh, no," thought James. They've forgotten my party."

James and Father went to the mall. "Look, James! Happy Birthday," said Father. Mother and all his friends were waiting at the Bunny King Burger Bar.

"Fantastic. A burger birthday party. My favorite."

Whenever Amy asked if there really were such things as giants, everyone would say, "No, only in fairy tales."

One day, Amy came running into the yard. "There are giants, there are! I've just seen them on TV." At first, her friends didn't believe her. "Come and see for yourselves," said Amy. So they all went indoors to look at the giants.

When they saw the pictures on TV, all her friends agreed. There really were giants. But they live far away in a place called Australia. That is why nobody had ever seen the giants.

Then Amy rushed into the kitchen. "I've seen giants. I've seen giants on TV!" Her father looked doubtful. "Are you sure?"

"Yes," said Amy. "It was a nature program. There were giant rabbits as tall as people. They jumped and ran very fast."

"Hmm," said Amy's father, looking very puzzled.

"They really were giant rabbits. And they carried their babies in a pocket at the front."

Father began to smile. "Why, Amy," he laughed. "Those aren't giant rabbits. They're kangaroos!"

Joanne and her friends were playing hide-and-seek. She was looking for somewhere to hide.

Suddenly Joanne found a big cabbage patch. She was very excited. Her friends would be pleased with her.

"Come here, come here," Joanne shouted. Everyone came running to see what all the fuss was about.

"Great," said Rufus, who was always hungry. "Let's see who can eat the most cabbage in ten minutes. On your mark. Get set. Go." So they all began eating the cabbage as fast as they could.

"Look out," said Rufus, "here comes Farmer Peters. Don't let him catch us!" Everyone turned on their tails and ran home as fast as they could.

Joanne's mother was waiting. "Where have you been?" Joanne told her all about their adventure. "Why did Farmer Peters chase us?" she asked.

"Well," said Mother, "he'd grown those cabbages especially for his pigs. They weren't there for you to eat."

"Oh, dear," said Joanne. "Never mind. We won't do it again."

"I've eaten too much. I feel sick," groaned Rufus.

"I'll NEVER eat another cabbage again."

It was Christmas Eve in Buniton, and all the little rabbits were singing carols with Miss Carrotly, the school teacher. Mr. Edward Bunworth's little house was the last place they came to. As they approached the house they could see that all the lights were off.

"Do you think he's home?" asked Jane.

"Maybe he's asleep," suggested Robin.

"We'll knock gently and sing quietly," said Miss Carrotly. Suddenly all the lights lit up, and the door flew open. There, in the doorway, stood an old rabbit, with a long white beard, and a red hat and cape.

"Ho! Ho! Ho!" he cried. "I'm Santa Bunny! Come in. I've got Christmas pies and cakes for everyone."

Jane and Robin Rabbit let the others go in first.

"Where's Edward?" asked Jane.

"Is he ill?" asked Robin.

Santa Bunny pulled off his false beard and red hat, and there was Edward!

"I borrowed Santa Bunny's clothes for tonight. Will you keep my secret from the others?" They nodded and followed "Santa" back to the party.

ohn Bunny was a builder. He built houses and cottages, and walls and fences, and every Saturday he and his wife Becky went for a drive in the country.

One Saturday, as they were driving through narrow country lanes, they came upon four young rabbits trying to pile up stones at the side of the road.

"What are you doing?" asked John Bunny.

"We're trying to build a wall to stop Farmer Brown's cows from getting into mother's vegetable patch," said the eldest little rabbit. "But it keeps falling down."

"It's a good thing I came along," said John, getting his tools from the car. "I'll give you a helping paw."

"Thank you very much," chorused the little rabbits.

So John Bunny showed the four little rabbits how to place the stones on top of each other so that they wouldn't fall down. Soon they had built a strong wall.

"There," said John. "All done." And he put his tools away.

"Goodbye," said the little rabbits. "And thank you."

Poor John was so tired that Becky had to drive them home again.

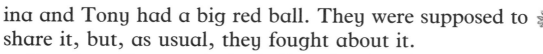

Tina and Tony had a big red ball. They were supposed to share it, but, as usual, they fought about it.

One day, Tony took the ball to the river bank.

Tina followed him and said, "Give me that ball."

"No!" said Tony, and he kicked it into the river.

"Now look what you've done!" said Tina. They both sat on the bank and looked glumly at the ball, which was slowly drifting downstream.

Otteline the otter came by.

"How did it get into the water?" she asked.

"We were fighting," said Tina.

"As usual," sighed Otteline. "I'll get the ball for you, if you promise not to fight any more."

The two bunnies promised.

Otteline fetched the ball and tossed it to Tina — who almost ran off with it. But she remembered the promise.

"Let's play together," she said. "It's more fun."

And it was.

The pile of soil appeared in the field quite suddenly, as if by magic.

Emmeline told the other bunnies there was probably a dragon under the heap. She poked a stick into it. Then she put her ear to the ground and listened.

She heard a shuffling, snuffling noise.

"It's definitely a dragon," she said.

"Oooh!" said the other bunnies.

The pile of soil began to move, and there was more scuffling and snuffling. "The dragon's coming up!" shouted Emmeline.

A minute later, a velvet face appeared through the earth. It was Algernon the mole, and he was very cross.

"Who poked that stick into my front room?" he demanded.

But there was no one there to answer him. All the little bunnies had scampered away, convinced they'd just missed being eaten by a dragon.

THE PAINTER

Sally Lopears was painting in her room. She spread a large piece of paper on the floor, got out her paints and brushes, and set to work.

First she painted the blue sky. Then she painted the green fields and a house. Last, she painted her mother standing beside the house.

When she was finished, she called out, "Mom, come and see what I've done!"

Mrs. Lopears went upstairs to Sally's room. When she looked inside, she saw the painting. And then she saw Sally!

"That's a nice picture," she said. "But you've got paint *all over* yourself. It's into the bath with you." She picked Sally up and put her into a nice, hot bubble bath.

"Tomorrow," said Sally, as her mother scrubbed her clean. "Tomorrow I shall paint a ship on the sea."

"Then please remember to wear your smock," sighed Mrs. Lopears. "Then you can paint on the paper and not on yourself.

"Yes, Mom," said Sally, splashing her bath water.

THE PUDDLE

It was raining hard as Terry was coming home from school. He was wearing a blue slicker and green boots and carrying a large red umbrella.

Terry was splashing in all the puddles. He liked splashing in puddles. He would take three long strides and then three short strides. Then he would jump SPLASH!, right in the middle of a big puddle. But, because of his slicker and boots, he did not get wet.

Just outside his house, there was a really big puddle. Terry stopped and looked at it for a long while. Then he took three long strides, and then three short strides, and jumped.

SPLASH! The water went everywhere. But Terry had lost his balance, and SPLASH! he sat down heavily, right in the middle of the puddle.

Water ran into his boots and into his slicker, and even into his pockets.

So it was a very wet bunny indeed who went home that afternoon. He decided that he would never ever splash in puddles again.

Chris liked to collect treasures. She collected bright things, colored beads, and pearls.

She had a secret hiding place for her treasures. It was in the backyard. Next to a rosebush she had made a hole, and her treasures were buried there.

When everyone was out, Chris would dig up her treasures. She would polish them. Sometimes she would swap beads with her friend, but mostly she just looked at her jewels.

One day, Chris woke up early. "It's cold today," she thought. It was snowing. "I won't be able to look at my treasures. I'll have to wait until it stops snowing."

When the snow stopped, Chris went outside. She looked everywhere for her treasures. She made lots of holes all over the yard, but she couldn't find them. The snow had hidden everything.

"Why are there so many holes in the yard?" asked Father sternly. Chris had a big tear in her eye. "I've lost my treasures. I've looked everywhere."

"Don't worry," said Father. "We'll find them when the snow melts."

And they did.

Today was Bobby Bunny's birthday. He had been looking forward to it all week long and inviting all of his friends to his house for a celebration.

When the time finally came for the party, and all his friends arrived at his house, Bobby's mother came into the dining room carrying an enormous birthday cake, decorated with five candles. Can you guess how old Bobby was?

Bobby was determined to blow out his candles by himself, and he huffed and puffed until they were all out. All his friends cheered and sang "Happy Birthday" to Bobby, who was smiling and laughing, and each gave him a small birthday present. Then his mother cut the cake and gave a slice to all the bunnies around the table. It was delicious!

"I made a wish when I blew out my candles," said Bobby. "I wished that every day could be as good as a birthday day."

Basil Bunny and his friends were playing hide and seek. Basil found a hiding place under some brambles at the edge of the wood.

He hid for a long time, but no one found him. He stayed hidden. It began to get dark, and Basil was a little bit frightened. There were moving shadows outside, and snuffling noises.

The noises outside got louder, and he heard footsteps. He stayed as still as he could.

Then he heard a voice he knew. "Basil!" it called.

"Dad!" cried Basil and bounced out of his hiding place. "I was so frightened!"

"I'm not surprised," said his dad, giving him a big hug. "The wood's no place for a bunny to be after dark. There are badgers and foxes and goodness knows what out at night. Come on, let's go home!"

And Basil trotted off after his dad, home to where his mom had a great big bowl of vegetable soup waiting just for him.

Timmy was a clever young bunny. He had been going to school for a few months, and today was the day he was going to learn how to write his name.

The whole class had been learning letters. Timmy could now write each letter, but he did not know how to make them into words. This was going to be a very special day.

"Everyone get out your paper and pencil," said the teacher, Miss Fluff. Timmy had a brand-new pencil. It was green with red stripes. His mother had bought it specially for him when he started school. He had not told his mother how important today was to him; it was going to be a surprise.

Miss Fluff went around each person in turn. When she got to Timmy, he was very excited. She showed him how to spell out his name — T I M M Y. He copied the name and felt very proud — "that's me," he thought to himself. "Aren't I grand."

That night, he showed his mother and father what he had learned at school and wrote TIMMY all over a piece of paper. They were very pleased with him. His mother told him that he could have a writing pad of his very own. This meant that he could write his name as often as he wanted. And that was just what he did.

onathan, Stephen, and Timothy Rabbit were going to visit their grandpa, Edward Bunworth, deep in the woods.

They stopped in a clearing to eat some sandwiches. As they started to go, Jonathan said, "Who has the letter Mother gave us?"

The two little rabbits searched their pockets. Stephen looked in the picnic basket.

"It's gone!" exclaimed Timothy.

They searched the clearing and each other again, but the letter was nowhere to be seen.

Grandpa was waiting at the rickety gate when they arrived. "Why so sad?" he asked.

"We had a letter for you," Stephen explained.

"But we lost it," Jonathan added sadly.

"I think someone stole it!" Timothy exclaimed.

"How big was this letter?" asked Grandpa.

"About as big as my paw," said Jonathan.

"And how heavy was this letter?" asked Grandpa.

"Not heavy at all," said Stephen.

"Was it light enough for Timothy to carry in the band of his hat?" asked Grandpa, bending down to pluck the letter from Timothy's hat.

"You are silly bunnies," chuckled Grandpa. "It was here all the time."

Johnny and his sister Flora were on their way to the fair. It had come to town a few days earlier, and they were really excited about going. They had never been to a fair before, you see.

From their house, they had been able to see the bright lights shining for days. What fun they were going to have!

Their mother gave them both some money to spend. They had enough for two rides each. Their mother told them to be very careful with it.

At the fair, they looked at the many rides to decide what to spend their money on. Would it be the merry-go-round, the ferris wheel, or the swings? Suddenly, Flora let out a cry. "What is the matter?" said her mother. "I've lost the money you gave me," sobbed Flora, "I must have dropped it. Now I won't be able to go on any of the rides."

Johnny looked at all the wonderful rides. "You can have half my money," he told Flora, "and we can go on a ride together." And that is just what they did. And do you know what their mother did? Because Johnny had not been selfish with his money, she bought him and Flora an ice cream each. They did have a fun day out after all.

It was getting later and later and later, and still Elizabeth couldn't get to sleep. In fact, it got so late that she heard her mom, then her dad, come to bed. Then she heard an owl hoot. She wondered what would happen to her if she stayed awake all night. She must have said this out loud, because, suddenly, a large green bird appeared by her bed and said, "Bunnies *always* fall asleep sooner or later."

"Bet I won't," said Elizabeth.

Suddenly, an enormous silver crocodile and an orange moth appeared by her bed.

"What happens to bunnies who stay awake all night?" asked Elizabeth.

"Bunnies *always* fall asleep sooner or later," said the crocodile.

"Bet I won't," said Elizabeth.

Suddenly, her mother was drawing back the curtains and saying, "Time to get up, Elizabeth." It was morning already!

"Mom, I think I've been awake all night," said Elizabeth.

Her mother laughed. "I don't think you have. Not unless you snore when you're awake."

Elizabeth thought about this. "In that case, not being able to sleep must have all been a dream!" she laughed. "What funny things dreams are."

Joe stood on the river bank looking down at the water. He could see fish swim in and out of the reeds as they played hide and seek. Joe wished he could be a fish. How much more fun it would be to get wet and splash about all day than doing boring, rabbit-type things on dry land. The trouble was, he couldn't swim.

Joe leaned over farther to see what the fish were up to, and SPLASH! he fell in. Ugh, how cold the water was. And how slimy the weeds felt. He coughed and spluttered. Luckily, his paws could reach the bottom, or he would have almost certainly drowned. As he climbed out, he could hear the fish laughing at him.

Poor Joe had to walk home cold, wet, and bedraggled, with green weeds hanging from his fur and tail. Perhaps he didn't want to be a fish after all.

His mother put him in a warm bath. "I'm going to arrange some swimming lessons for you," she said. "You can still pretend to be a fish if you want to, but in the comfort of a swimming pool, where the lifeguards can keep an eye on you and no slimy weeds will get in your way."

"Oh, thanks, Mom," said Joe. And it wasn't long before he could swim like — yes — a fish!

Ricky Rabbit and his friends decided to have a contest. The first event was to climb up an old tree. Ricky found it harder to do than he expected. He had only gotten a short distance off the ground, when his arms ached so much he had to get down.

Then Sam Squirrel had a turn. He raced up and down the tree in no time. "I win!" he called. "Squirrels are very good at climbing!"

"Now let's find out who can hang upside down the longest!" said Bert the Bat. You can guess who won, can't you? After all, bats do that all the time. The third event was to see who could hide the longest without the others finding him. This time, Marty Mouse won, because mice are smaller than rabbits and not seen so easily.

By now, only Ricky hadn't won anything.

"Wait a minute!" he called. "Why don't we have a HOPPING race?"

This time, Ricky won easily. For as you know, of course, rabbits can *hop* very, very well.

Funny Bunny thought he was very funny. He was always playing tricks on his friends. Of course, they were harmless. But his friends were getting fed up with him.

"Duck!" he shouted to his brother by the pond.

"Why?" replied his brother, bending down quickly and looking startled.

"I meant, Daisy Duck!" giggled Funny Bunny. "Ha-ha-ha! There she goes—flying across the pond!"

So the tricks went on. Until, one day, Funny Bunny saw lots of his friends calling him.

"Have a look through Fergus Fox's telescope!" said Funny Bunny's brother. "It's really funny!"

"Why?" said Funny Bunny, who couldn't see anything funny at all. Then everyone began to laugh at him. Funny Bunny was so surprised he ran home to find out why. When he peered in the mirror, there was a black mark all around his eye.

"It's only grease!" said his brother, coming to find him. "It will easily wipe off! I TOLD you it was funny! Hee-hee!"

But Funny Bunny didn't laugh—and he never played another trick again.

W hy are you called Rattle?" one rabbit asked another.

"Come with me and I'll show you," said Rattle. He went home and took some dried beans out of a bag in the kitchen. He placed them in a plastic jar and put a lid on top.

"See?" said Rattle.

But the other rabbit shook his head. Then Rattle began to shake the jar, so all the dried beans rattled around. What a noise they made!

"Stop! stop!" cried the other rabbit, holding his ears.

"I like to rattle things!" grinned Rattle. "By the way, what is your name?"

"Squirt," replied the other rabbit, smiling. "Do you want to know why?"

"I think I can guess," said Rattle. "You like to squirt a water pistol!"

"No," said Squirt, pointing to a flower he was wearing on his jacket. Puzzled, Rattle peered closely at the flower; the next moment, a jet of water shot out from it and splashed him.

"I like to squirt my *trick* flower!" chuckled Squirt. Now Rattle laughed, too.

Meg was afraid of the dark, so her brother gave her a special nightlight to keep on all night.

Meg didn't like the nightlight. She lay in bed and looked around. She was scared. She began to cry, and her mother came into her room to ask, "What's the matter?"

"There are ghosts in here!" sobbed Meg.

"They're not ghosts," said her mother. "They're just shadows. You can make shadow birds—look!"

She showed Meg how to hold her paws in front of the light and make bird-shaped shadows on the wall.

"That's a big, friendly bird," said her mother. "Can you make any other animals? Try and see."

Meg's mother kissed her goodnight and left her alone. Meg sat up in bed and tried making more animals. Then she made some ghosts, too, but she wasn't afraid of them, because she'd made them herself.

And then she curled up and went to sleep.

Simon Bunny was sad, because all the other bunnies in his class had special sneakers, and he had no sneakers at all, only an old pair of brown shoes.

"These brown shoes are boring," said Simon. "I want sneakers."

"We can't afford new sneakers just yet," said his mother. "You can have some later."

"I want them now!" said Simon. "I hate my boring old brown shoes!"

That night, he went to sleep and dreamed about new sneakers. In the morning, he looked for his boring brown shoes. But he couldn't find them anywhere.

Instead, he found some bright red shoes, complete with yellow laces.

"I dyed them for you and got new laces," explained his mother. "I know they aren't sneakers, but they're not boring now, are they?"

"They're wonderful," said Simon. "They're better than sneakers! Sneakers are boring!"

Ethel didn't like her new school, because she didn't know any of the other bunnies and she had no special friend of her own. When playtime came, she sat in a corner and looked miserable. If any other bunnies came near her, she said, "Go away!"

After a while, another little bunny sat down near her. The other bunny looked miserable, too. At first, Ethel didn't say anything.

The other bunny didn't say anything, either.

Then Ethel said, "Why are you sitting here?"

"I'm lonely," said the other bunny. "I'm new here. I haven't got anyone to play with. I want a special friend of my own."

"So do I," said Ethel.

"Then we'd better be friends," said the other bunny, jumping up. "Come on, let's play! My name's Alice; what's yours?"

"Ethel," said Ethel. "What shall we play?"

And that was how Ethel found a special friend.

Arabella Rabbit's most important possession was her magic cupboard. It was all she needed. If she wanted anything at all—clothes, or food, or new curtains—she just whispered a magic spell through the keyhole, opened the cupboard, and there it was.

Gregory Bunny was jealous. He planned and plotted, and one day while Arabella was out, he came in his truck and took the cupboard away.

Then he muttered all the magic words he knew into the keyhole and said: "Give me a special surprise!"

He said that because now that he had the cupboard, he couldn't think of anything he wanted.

The cupboard certainly gave him a surprise. It opened its doors and grabbed Gregory by the ears. Then it flew into the air and soared over the duck pond, where it dropped him with a great big splash.

After that, it flew home and was back in its corner before Arabella ever knew it had been away.

Nan Rabbit hated taking Baby to the supermarket, because he always cried.

"Please don't cry," said Nan, but Baby always did.

Nan tried giving him toys, but he still cried. She tried telling him a story, but he still cried. She tried singing to him, but he still cried.

It was no good. Baby just hated going shopping.

One day, Nan said, "Sorry Baby, but I'm afraid we've got to go to the supermarket."

Baby cried all the time, until Nan bought a pink feather duster.

Baby stopped crying and stared at the duster.

He grabbed it, he waved it about, he tickled his own face and giggled. Nan pushed the cart around the supermarket, and Baby waved and tickled and giggled all the way.

After that, whenever Nan went shopping with Baby, they always took the pink duster.

And Baby never cried again.

When winter came, the bunnies didn't go out.

The rain poured down, and a cold wind blew. The ground was muddy, and the sky was dark. When the bunnies woke up in the morning, everywhere was gloomy and gray, and it stayed like that all day.

"We hate winter!" said the young bunnies. "We want summer to come again—quickly!"

Then, one morning, there seemed to be an odd, white light coming through their bedroom window. They looked out. The whole world was white.

"It's snow!" they cried. They put on their boots and their scarves and their hats and rushed outside.

All day they made snow rabbits and igloos and had snowball fights.

When evening came, they went indoors. They were cold and tired, but they'd had a wonderful day.

"We love winter!" they said. "We don't want summer to come again—ever!"

They call me Boxing Bunny!" said a bunny to his friend, Seth Squirrel, when they met in the street.

"Why?" asked Seth, puzzled.

In answer, Boxing Bunny began to punch the air with his paws. "Can't you guess?" said Boxing Bunny.

"No," said Seth, "and what are you doing that for?"

Boxing Bunny started to hop around lightly and swing his paws all the more.

"I'm going down to the gym to practice," said Boxing Bunny. "Surely, you can guess now?"

Before Boxing Bunny could say that he was training to be a famous boxer, Seth saw Sarah Squirrel step out of a store, carrying lots and lots of boxes.

"Look out, Boxing Bunny!" said Seth. But Boxing Bunny stepped back and bumped into her, by mistake. He knocked all the boxes out of her hands.

"S. . .sorry, Sarah," said Boxing Bunny, picking them up. "At least let me take these home for you."

"Now I know why you're named Boxing Bunny," cried Seth. "You're carrying those *boxes*!"

CARROT CRAZY

"I'm going to open a restaurant," Rita Rabbit told her friend, Sarah Squirrel. "Would you like to help me run it?"

"Yes, please!" said Sarah, who enjoyed cooking.

So, on the opening night, Sarah was all set in the kitchen. When the first customers arrived, Rita greeted them and took their orders. Then she ran into the kitchen.

"One carrot soup and one carrot cake, please, Sarah," called Rita.

"Coming up in no time!" replied Sarah, who set to work to cook them.

More customers arrived and sat at the tables, and Rita took their orders, too.

"One carrot juice and a carrot pie, please, Sarah," she called into the kitchen.

Soon, the restaurant was full.

"Another carrot salad and some carrot crunchies, Sarah!" said Rita, while her friend kept on cooking busily.

"I'm getting fed up just cooking with carrots," said Sarah Squirrel, who was so busy she had not stepped out of the kitchen all evening. "Why don't your customers eat anything but carrots?"

"Didn't I tell you?" said Rita.
"This is a *restaurant for rabbits*!"

"I like running," said a young rabbit, as he raced round and round his dad's backyard.

"Well, don't run on my nice green lawn. You'll wear it out!" said Dad.

"You can run into town and do my shopping for me," called Mom.

"Great!" said Running Rabbit, taking the shopping list, some money, and a bag. But he had not gone far when the streets were so busy that Running Rabbit had to slow down to a gentle jog.

"Where *can* I run?" Running Rabbit asked his mom.

"Where you won't get in anyone's way," said his mother. So Running Rabbit ran across a field.

"Hey! Shoo!" called the farmer. "I've just planted that field with carrot seed!"

"Oo. . .er! Sorry! I didn't know!" called Running Rabbit, who ran home once more and ran upstairs into his bedroom.

Thud! THUD! **THUD!** His mother heard a steady thumping noise as she worked in the kitchen below. She went to see what her son was up to now.

"I like running on the spot best of all!" he told her, puffing and out of breath.

RACER RABBIT

Racer Rabbit rode a BMX bike. He could do all sorts of tricks on it. He wore a helmet and special clothes to protect himself in case he fell off. But he never did. He was the best rider at the BMX track.

Soon his friends refused to race against him because he always won. Racer began to boast so much the others wished that, just once, someone would be better on a bike. But there was not much chance of that!

One day, a new rabbit came to live in town. His name was Rider.

"I'll bet you can't ride a bike as well as I can!" said Racer, doing his tricks on his BMX bike.

"I bet you can't ride *my* bike," said Rider.

"Oh, yes, I can!" boasted Racer.

So Rider went to fetch it. When he returned, Racer and his friends stared. Rider was balancing on a bicycle that only had one wheel!

"It's called a *unicycle*!" said Rider. "I ride it in my parents' circus! Would you like to try?"

"N. .no, thanks," said Racer, riding off, while everyone else chuckled.